THE ARRANGEMENT
By Tyrone Newburn

Chapter 1

I0521187

On a early Wednesday morning, you can hear the birds chirping away through a opened window in the kitchen. The aroma of freshly brewed coffee permeates the entire house. Tony, sitting at the kitchen table, waits for his loving wife Cora to pour him a cup. She pours the coffee, then stands behind her husband, gently rubbing his shoulders."Baby..........again I want to say thank you for being so understanding......and patient with me through this problem I'm ha..... " Tony abruptly replies "Sweetheart.... like I said last night, I'm in this for better and for worse. You don't have to keep apologizing. How long have we known each other Cora?" "Since the third grade." "That's right, about 40 years. " "Who's counting! "Cora jokingly replied. "Even though we're going through a rough patch......sexually, I still love you more than ever.......I mean that Cora." "Thank you baby, and I love you too." She says as she stops rubbing his shoulders and reaches down to kiss him on the earlobe. While Cora was in close proximity of Tony's ear, she asks softly "Have you thought more about what we've discussed last night?" Tony slowly inhaled then exhaled and answers "Yes....I thought about it....I thought about it half the night."

Last night after an unsuccessful attempt to have sexual intimacy [and there were many failed attempts during the last three years] Tony cuddled and kissed his wife as though they had made passionate love. He knew Cora felt bad about the situation, and didn't want her to worry about it any more than necessary. Cora was diagnosed with multiple sclerosis thirty years ago. Her symptoms has gotten progressively worse throughout the years. Often times she uses a cane, which sometimes makes her feel not-so-good about herself. But Cora has always been open to new sexual experiences. She's been going to a sex therapist for two years, but nothing seems to be working. Cora very much wants her husband to be pleased. As they lie in bed, Cora's head was still resting on Tony's chest. She asks "baby...um....what's your fantasy? I mean what do you fantasize about?"

"Wow......hum....fantasy? Baby, I don't think you'd want to know. You may think of me differently once I tell you. Besides, why do you want to know my fantasies?" Tony asked with fascination. Cora subserviently replied "I'm just interested in knowing what might please you...my dear husband." " Well baby.....there's one fantasy I have........ I fantasize having a lady friend......one who can be a friend as well as a lover.....with your approval of course. Also I would want this woman to be your friend......kinda like a second wife.....the three of us would work as a team. That's my fantasy. " Cora went silent for about 15 seconds and then responded "I can work with that." As if he couldn't believe what he was hearing, Tony asked "are you for real? " With a sincere look on her face and in her voice, Cora responds "yes....yes I am. We can have a friend...... upon my approval.....ok? " Tony softly answered " Yes, thanks. "

"Tony, how much sugar are you going to put in your coffee? " "Oh, look at me....I'm sorry. Between your warm hands on my shoulder and the kiss on my earlobe, I guess I got carried away. " Cora smiles and then took her seat at the kitchen table. As she stirs her coffee, looking eye to eye Cora asks "So.....you thought about this half the night huh? " "Yeah, I did. This is a fascinating concept to say the least. I must say, it kinda blew my mind. It takes a selfless woman to agree with something like this. I think that's one of the reasons why I love you so much.........another reason is, you can COOK! " They both laughed as Cora shakes her head side to side. "But seriously Cora..... I'd like to get back with you on this. " "Sure, take as much time as you need. " Tony looks at his watch, gives his wife a peck on the lips and says "I don't want to be late for work. I'll see you at choir rehearsal okay? " "See ya honey. " As Cora continued drinking her coffee.

After work , Tony sat in his car for a while to gather his thoughts. Then he remembers the new choir member who he met two years ago at Thursday night Bible study class. Her name is Crystal. For the past two years, Tony noticed that this young lady would stare at him almost constantly . On many occasions, she would even sit next to him in class. When it comes to intelligence, she seems well beyond her years. Tony and Crystal eventually exchanged cell phone numbers and would correspond from time to time via text message. He received a phone call from Crystal while at work one day. She seemed a bit nervous but asked if it's okay if she can call him sometime. He agreed,and then asked her if she could join him for coffee at the Starbucks in Hyde park. Crystal enthusiastically agreed. That same day, while at Starbucks, Crystal nervously asked Tony if they can take their relationship to the next level. Tony seemed a little puzzled, then asked Crystal for clarification on "next level ". She replied "out to dinner, to the movies. " Tony smiles and says "on to the next level. " Shortly after the "next level "conversation, Crystal joins the sanctuary choir. " The age differences [Tony 54, Crystal 27] didn't seem to matter to the two of them. Tony suspected that Crystal wanted more out of the relationship than just a friendship.

Tony pulls into the Ridgeway Baptist church parking lot, the church where he and Cora attends and sings in the choir. Tony is a half hour early for rehearsal so he sits in his car debating whether to inform Cora of his choice. He thought about it all day at work and the only woman he could come up with was Crystal. To Tony, Crystal appeared to be the only one besides Cora sexually interested in him. Tony felt a bit apprehensive about what might be Cora's reaction, but decided on Crystal.

And then Cora pulled into a parking spot along side Tony. When Cora got out of her car, Tony gestured for her to get in. She got in, then gave him a peck on the lips and says "Hey baby, what's going on? " "Well babe......uh.....I think I found that....um...friend. "Wow baby, that was fast! " Cora says with amazement. "Well she's actually a good friend that you and I both know. She's a member of our church and you seemed to get along with her very well. " "I know her? Cora asked. "Yes you do Cora. " "Well who is she? " "If you will allow me, I'd like to inform you after dinner and a movie on Saturday. " Resisting her curiosity, Cora agreed on a date for Saturday.
"Let's get this rehearsal over with " Tony says before they exited the car. Cora agrees.

As Tony and Cora enters the sanctuary, most of the choir members were seated in the loft. Cora took her place in the Sopranos section and Tony sat of course with the tenors. As Tony said his hellos, his eyes caught Crystals. He'd still catch Crystal staring from time to time. He also found himself staring.
Tony had to be discreet because Crystal mostly sat next to his wife. But unbeknownst to Crystal and Tony, there was another set of eyes watching the both of them stare at each other. That set of

eyes belonged to Rosie Sanchez. On a scale from 1 to 10, Rosie was 20. The Puerto Rican beauty had been watching Tony for quite a while now. When Rosie began noticing Tony staring at Crystal, she started to put together a plan and she knew it was time to make her move because she wasn't going to let this one escape. You see, Rosie has issues, serious issues. Dad left her at the age of 10. Her fiancé left her at the alter at 21 and at 34 her best male friend announced his nuptials to a long time friend. Rosie had just realized she loved her male friend more than she thought. She was so crushed. Rosie prayed and prayed and even demanded that God intervene. Rosie then snapped, vowing to find that special man before here 37th birthday, before her biological clock runs out. Although Rosie is extremely pretty, most men she met were intimidated by her well educated persona, put off by her clingyness and she showed mistrust in most men.

Tony and Cora are cuddled-up in their bed after a wonderful night out. They've just made love [real love, with all the bells and whistles] for the first time in quite a while. They laid there, laughing and discussed the play [Tyler Perry's Madea Gets A Job] they had enjoyed that night. They both loved the concert performance that was at the end of the play. Cora particularly loved the restaurant Tony recommended [Asian Harbors] in south suburban Homewood, Illinois. Cora marveled at the restaurants decor and ambiance. She thanked Tony for a wonderful evening. Then the inevitable question surfaced. "So ah.........who's the lucky woman who will serve as your bed mate? With the look of confidence on his face Tony responded "Crystal " Cora pauses for a few seconds and asks "Which Crystal are you talking about? I know of two Crystal's. Crystal Brown is in Wichita Kansas, and the only other Crystal I know is the Crystal in the choir. " "Yep, that's her. " Tony says with confidence. "But she's so young! " says the stunned Cora. Tony then began to sell his choice to his wife. He told her how they met, that she would stare at him almost constantly, that they would meet for coffee on a couple of occasions, and that Crystal expressed a willingness to take their relationship to the "next level ". Tony speculated that Crystal wanted more than she let on. He also emphasizes that this young woman is moldable and impressionable and will do well in this situation. Tony stressed that if Cora accepts his choice, she'd never have to worry about him leaving her for Crystal. Cora asks for a couple of minutes to think and to ponder on what Tony had brought to the table. Cora sat on the side of the bed and appeared to be in deep thought. Tony, still laying in the bed with his hands behind his head, stares cautiously at Cora. She then stood up and says " I gotta use it ". When Cora got to the bathroom, she close the door then leaned on it and looked up and asked "I hope I'm doing the right thing" Cora sat on the toilet and debated the pros and cons, and the morality of allowing her husband to sleep with another woman. The main concern Cora had was that Crystal might steal her husband, everything else she could handle.

Cora returned from the bathroom and sat on the side of the bed next to her husband. She fondly looked at her husband while holding his hand. "Cora........before you speak, I'd like to say.....again......I will never leave you. And, I appreciate you on being so open-minded about this sort of thing. I know it must be hard to even consider this. If....at any time Cora, you need to step back from this, I will understand.....and respect your wishes. " Cora looked down at their embraced hands and then looked into her husbands eyes and says softly " Baby....let's go for it. But there needs to be some ground rules....okay? " Tony agreed, and then Cora laid down what she thought would be good ground rules for this arrangement. She asked Tony to arrange a meeting between the three of them as soon as possible.

Tony began to develop a stronger relationship with the nervous and shy Crystal. First by staying in contact via the cell phone, going on dates to coffee shops, meetings at the multiplex theater and any place they can talk and feel each other out.

On a late evening date to the multiplex in Orland Park, Crystal expressed interest in expanding their friendship to a bi-exclusive relationship. Tony immediately made it clear that his wife was open to the idea of him having a girl on the side but that she had to have a meeting with Cora to give the final ok. Crystal not only sweated bullets at the thought of his wife knowing about the affair, but having a face to face with her was almost unbearable. But Crystal reluctantly agreed. Tony then asked Crystal to meet them after Sundays service at Rudy's soulful restaurant.

After worship service the following Sunday, Cora and Tony went to their favorite soul food restaurant to have a brunch/ meeting with Crystal. Five minutes later Crystal nervously walked into the restaurant, spots the waiting couple and told the maître d' that she was with the couple seated in the corner. Crystal was nervously shaking as she sat down. Noticing Crystal was shaking, Cora reached out and touched Crystal's hand to assure her that everything would be alright. After expressing the awkwardness of the meeting, Cora got down to meat of the conversation. She told Crystal that this arrangement must be on the down-low and that all bets are off if it became noticeable to anyone. She was also informed Crystal that she had to take an AIDS test and practice safe sex at all times. Most importantly, Crystal had to agree not to attempt to lure Tony away from her. Crystal was mostly silent as Cora explained the ground rules to her. "Are you all ready to order? " the waiter asked. They made their orders and continued the conversation. Cora ask Crystal if she had any questions or concerns regarding what they had talked about so far. "No......I think you covered just about everything ". Crystal says with a shaky voice. At the end of the meal, Cora invited Crystal to go on a shopping date [to develop a deeper friendship and to school the young inexperience Crystal], she agrees. Cora and her counterpart exchanged phone numbers and agreed to meet at the River Oaks shopping mall on the next day.

While at the shopping mall, Cora and Crystal seem to be getting along nicely. They walked throughout the mall like 30yr friends that had just reunited. They had lunch together and seemed genuinely happy to be in each others company. Cora had even purchased a gift for Crystal. Everything seem to come together nicely for the two of them. At the end of their shopping date they made a promise to one another to keep the focus on Tony's sexual needs.

During Wednesday choir rehearsal Cora and Crystal, singing in the soprano section, glances at one another with an air of fondness. Tony, singing with the tenor, watches both of them, eagerly waiting for the next get-together with Crystal. As the choir exited the choir loft, Rosie, who sings alto nudges Tony in the lower back, thanking him again for changing her tire a week prior. Tony answered, "it was no problem Rosie, anytime you need help, just let me know". Rosie replied with a smile "I will.....oh by the way Tony, you left your jacket in my car after you changed the tire". Tony wondered what happened to that jacket. Rosie told Tony he could pick up his jacket tomorrow before she take a flight to Puerto

Rico. Tony agreed to pick up the jacket before 7pm the next day.

It was a torrential rain storm that consumed all of Thursday. It was six thirty and the rain was coming down so heavy that Tony had to sit in his car and try to wait until the rain shower slows down. But the rain kept coming, so Tony decided to brave the rain and walk up the long flight of stairs to retrieve his jacket from Rosie. By the time Tony got to the top of the stairs he was soaking wet. Tony pushed the door bell, once,twice, then the door opened. There was Rosie, in a sexy two piece silk lounging outfit, black, dotted with medium red roses. "Hi Tony, oh you are soaking wet. Let me help you with this wet jacket"." I'm fine Rosie, I know you have to catch a flight soon". "My flight was canceled due to this terrible storm Tony, we have plenty of time. I rescheduled the flight for tomorrow night, plus I need to throw this wet jacket in the dryer....I insist".

Rosie took the jacket to the laundry room. When she came back, she asked Tony if he wanted to watch a movie she'd started watching before he rung the door bell. Rosie said she could use a little company because since childhood, she couldn't stand thunderstorms.

Then a large clap of thunder sounded and the lights flickered, then the power shuts down. With tears in her eyes, Rosie asked " can you stay for a little while? " Tony agrees to stay.

Tony sat down on the sofa, admiring the beautiful artwork on the walls. She had wonderful accent pieces throughout her home, tastefully placed. Rosie walked over to the portable bar, asked Tony if he would join her for a glass of wine. Now,Tony wasn't much of a drinker, but nods yes.

Rosie sat down on a white leather chase lounge, folding one leg under her butt and one leg folded upward. Like an eager child, Rosie began to ask questions about his career, college, childhood and anything she could think of to keep Tony on that sofa. Plus she kept Tony's glass full.

After a couple of hours Tony had a good buzz going, slurring his words and belching. Rosie got up from the chase lounge and sat next to Tony and continued talking for a few more minutes.

Then Rosie moved closer and slips between his right arm and torso. Rosie then began to softly rub Tony's right thigh as he continued to slur his words. At this time Rosie had him where she wanted him.

When Tony woke up he was laying in Rosie's king size bed. The clock on the wall read 1:15am. All he was wearing was his white v-neck tee shirt,boxers and sox. He can hear the shower running then suddenly shut off. His clothes, slacks and dry jacket were laid out across the bed. With his head pounding from the alcohol, Tony sat up on the side of the bed, rubbing his head and calling out for Rosie. Rosie appeared from the bathroom with a beautiful satin robe with her hair rapped in a bath towel. "Hey sleepy head, I dried your jacket". "How did I get here?". Tony asked. " You don't remember Tony?" she asked with a smirk on her face. "No......... I don't think so.......I vaguely remember.......no I think it was a dream..... it must have been the alcohol". Rosie told him she had took off his clothes as not to wrinkle them, and put him in her bed so that he could sleep off the alcohol. He then began to put on his clothes.

Tony looked at his watch, it had 1:30am. " Oh Lord, I have to go home. Thanks for everything Rosie...sorry I couldn't hold my alcohol, it don't take much for me". "that's ok, I enjoyed your company even while you slept" she said with a big smile. As Rosie opened the front door, she immediately gave Tony a firm hug, saying. "we must do this again".

Tony and Crystal embarked on a once a week rendezvous, usually to dinner and the movies. They seemed to get more comfortable with each other after each date. Tony sensed Crystal was more shy than she let on. Tony noticed early on that Crystal was extremely shy because she would perspire and tremble. Little did Tony know, Crystal had no experience with older men......and younger men for that matter. She had only one boyfriend in her short life, a thug who's only mission was to bed her down...if you know what I mean. One night the thug begged Crystal to have sex with him, when she nicely resisted, the thug tried to force himself on her. Crystal got away by kicking him in the family jewels...it was a close call for Crystal. She really never got over the trauma of being nearly raped.

Luckily for Crystal, Tony had the patience of Job. Tony realized that if he wanted to take Crystal to the next level, he would have to proceed slowly....after all, she's really a virgin.

After each encounter, progress would be made. First a kiss on the cheek, then a kiss on the mouth. Tony patiently taught Crystal how to French kiss. Once she got the hang of it, it was on! Crystal got horny every time they'd kiss, and Tony noticed. Her hands combed through his body like she was searching for the Crackerjack prize. Tony knew she was ready.

Crystal suggested they go to her place, where she shared an apartment with her sister, Crystal said her sister will be spending the night over their moms. Tony smiled and took her hand, driving slowly to her apartment. As Tony exited the car to open the door for his new lover, Crystal, with a nerves grin, extended her trembling hand to be helped out of his car. Tony could tell she was a bit overwhelmed so he hugged her while kissing under her right earlobe. He whispered "we"ll be just fine". They walked towards the apartment building, with his right arm clutching the ball if her shoulder. Crystal glances at her new lover with anticipation, nervously inhaling, then reached out with both hands for Tonys face. Then she kissed Tony passionately, her tong down his throat as though she was ready to experience whatever he had to offer. Crystal invited Tony inside her two bedroom flat and then slowly closed the door.

Two hours later, lying in Crystals bed, Tony looked over at his new and unbelievably pretty and sexy young lover. Crystal was curled up in the fetal position underneath Tonys arm. He couldn't believe he was with such a beautiful woman. Even with the drool running down the side her cheeks, dripping onto the pillow case, she was still fine as great wine. The aroma of their body chemistry was still lingering in the air. He also couldn't believe that Crystal was so submissive. Tony could tell right away she was green, a new-bee, but Crystal quickly learned how to follow Tonys lead. She was an eager student willing to do what it takes to satisfy her new lover. The trance-like stare she gave after each orgasm was reassuring to Tony and he knew she was getting more aroused on Tonys sexual ability.

At that moment, all Tony could think of is "thank God" for being so blessed with such a wonderful and openminded wife that would allow him to have a sexual partner on the side. While gazing at his sleeping nubian queen, Tony realized he must find a way to thank Cora for her graciousness and understanding on this matter.

Crystal began to wake-up, wiping the sleep from her eyes. She sat up, grabbed Tonys hand and asked "is everything fine." He answered "this is a beautiful thing Crystal, it's really wonderful".

She laid her head across his chest, smiled with an air of satisfaction on her face, and then closed her eyes.

Three month later, Tony and Cora's relationship is now better than ever. They had just come back from a seven day cruise to the Bahamas and Cora thanked her husband for a wonderful vacation, but Tony stopped Cora in mid-sentence to say "no Cora, thank you for being so understanding. I thank God everyday for giving me such a wonderful wife and friend". Cora now felt much better knowing she won't have pressure to preform sexually as much. Although Crystal had filled the gap sexually for Tony, Tony never stop trying to sexually please his wife. And Tony found different ways to make Cora sexually aroused. Facials and a little alcohol sometimes does the trick....[if you know what I mean].

Tony and Cora expressed their love for one-another constantly. They were always the best of friends as well as lovers, even more so now that they seem to have worked out their problem. Tony learned how to manage Crystals time without neglecting Cora....they would alternate on Fridays and Saturday's, early afternoons and late evenings to mix it up so that Cora would have a sense of unpredictability. So if Tony comes home three hours late Thursday or Friday or even Monday, Cora would think her husband was do something mundane....Cora tried to leave the back-of-the-mind stuff alone....as much as she could. As long as Cora's needs were being met and not neglected, she was just fine.

Crystal had to learn how to keep her emotions and adoration for Tony in check. You see, early in Tony and Crystals relationship, Tony started to notice Crystal being a bit clingy and possessive. Tony sat his young lover down and had a long and thoughtful discussion. Crystal was told that she had to keep her feelings, clingyness and possessiveness in check. And if it persisted, their relationship would be no more. Tony gave her a week to think about it. Time alone made Crystal put things in perspective. Crystal, with tears in her eyes, approached her well seasoned lover and apologized. It was extremely heartfelt. You know, Crystal was so apologetic, she was willing to cut down the number of days they would meet per month, or do whatever it takes to keep him. Crystal absolutely didn't want Cora to know about their misunderstanding.Crystal remembered what Cora had told her about keeping the focus on Tonys needs. Cora wanted to keep things on the down-low, and that all bets were off if it became noticeable. Crystal knew then she had dodged a bullet. From that point on, she was the perfect lover for Tony. His wish was her command. And when Crystal looked back at their relationship, she realized that she had been treated like a wife. She honestly admitted that in her apology to Tony. Crystal was treated well [like a Queen] by Tony.

While at choir rehearsal, Rosie was still watching Tony and Crystal stare at each other. She wondered to herself "what if Cora found out about that pretty young thang messing around with her husband....ummm". About three month ago, on a visit to her favorite restaurant, Rosie spotted Tony and Crystal sitting at a table in a dark secluded corner, eating, laughing and enjoying some cocktails. Rosie very much wanted to approach them, but unfortunately had to suddenly throw-up. Once Rosie finished with the puke, she took out her cell phone, then returned to her table and continued her surveillance. She discreetly videoed Tony and the young Crystal. She couldn't believe they were holding hands under the table. Rosie observed the couples interactions, watching everything they did. From the way they sampled from each other food, to the way they laughed and gazed at each other. She notice Crystal being very touchy feely during their conversation, making sure her touches lasts more than five seconds. It was obvious to Rosie that they were more than just friends.

Rosie could hardly wait for rehearsal to be over. She had a secret to tell Tony, and this secret not only could change his life, but could change the relationship he has between Cora and Crystal. Yes, Rosie is pregnant with Tonys baby and she is glad to be. All she could think about was how to break the good news, or in Tonys case the bad news about expecting his baby, and how to get Tony to leave his wife. You see, Rosie, had planned all along to get Tony so intoxicated that she would have her way with him....and she did! Yes....Rosie raped Tony. She raped him for two hours on that stormy and rainy night. She also videoed the rape as to make it look like Tony was a willing participant. The camera was positioned at Tonys feet to make it look like he was conscious of what he was doing...... but he was semi-conscious during the rape. Rosie's face could not be seen. She rode Tony like a race horse.

Rosie still had the jacket thatTony left in her car the day he changed her tire. You see, Tony left the jacket again because he was in a rush to leave after he woke up from being raped. After rehearsal Rosie planed on telling Tony once and for all to pick up his jacket....and then break the news of the pregnancy.

Finally.....rehearsal was over. While walking towards Tony, Rosie bumped into Crystal. They exchanged complements, then Crystal asked Rosie if she was picking up weight....or is it the clothes. Rosie replied with a big grin "girl, I'm pregnant ". Crystal congratulated Rosie on her pregnancy and asked her who's the lucky man. Rosie lowered her voice and said she'll tell her later, and that he is a member of the church. Crystal said ok and then walked over to where Cora and other friends were.

Rosie walked towards Tony, where he was talking with two male choir members....she waited patiently. Tony, noticing that Rosie was waiting, broke off the conversation with the guys and asked her how she was doing. She told him everything was fine, that things couldn't be better. She told Tony she was in a situation where she needed a male point of view, and could he stop by and discuss it with her, and to finally pick up his jacket, once and for all. Tony was agreeable and said he would be over tomorrow after work.

While Tony and Rosie talked, Crystal watched them intently. Noticing the glow on Rosie's face, Crystal concluded in her mind that something just wasn't right. At that moment, while Crystal was still staring, Rosie turned her eyes towards Crystal, staring back at her. The look on Rosie's face was unmistakably telling. Rosie looked as though she knew Crystal was aware that something was up. Then Cora broke away from her group and ask her husband if he is ready to go. Tony responded quickly and said yes. As he walked away, Crystal and Rosie was still locked in a stare that lasted about five seconds more, which was enough to let each other know that some toes were being stepped on. Crystal picked up her things and exited behind Cora and Tony. Rosie, watching Crystal walk out of the sanctuary with her lips pressed firmly together, inhaling deeply through her nose and holding her stomach. Rosie said to herself "I must find a away to break-up Crystal and Tonys relationship.... by any means necessary".

As Rosie walked towards her car, she began to mumble words resembling "gotta get them out the way", " Cora's gonna find out about Crystal....and Im going to make sure of it! It's going to be ugly y'all..... our baby needs a daddy". Once Rosie got into her car, she began to hyperventilate. She then reached for a empty zip-lock bag, then began breathing into it profusely. After about a minute she began to feel better, and then drove off.

The next day, Crystal phoned Tony during his lunch hour to invite him for cocktails at the local Chili's restaurant before he goes home, just to touch bases. Tony accepted her invitation but cautioned her that two drinks is his maximum because he can't hold his liquor, and the last time he went overboard, he woke up in some woman's bed. Crystal pressed Tony on who was the woman but Tony said he is somewhat embarrassed at the whole situation. Crystal said they could talk about this later over a couple drinks. Tony agreed.

Tony then realized he had made a promise to stop by Rosie's place. He told Crystal it had totally slipped his mind that he had to pick up something at Rosie Sanchez's place, but they could meet about an hour later. Crystals curiosity peeked big time. Knowing Rosie maybe up to no good, Crystal quickly asked Tony if he wanted her to pick up what ever it was from Rosie. Tony thanked her and said he really appreciate the offer, but Rosie also wanted to talk about something. Crystal knew then she had to do something.......but she didn't know what that something was.

An hour later, Crystal phoned Rosie and asked her if she wanted free samples from Avon. Crystal sold Avon products part time and had many choir members as clients. She knew free stuff would get her through Rosie's front door. Rosie took the bait and agreed to meet her at five pm. Crystal immediately drove to Babies R Us to purchase a baby monitor, the new compact version, to plant in Rosie's apartment.

At four fifty five, Crystal pulls up in front of Rosie's apartment building. She takes a deep breath before exiting her vehicle. With bags in her hands, Crystal walked up the stairs of the grey stone three flat and rang the bell. About ninety seconds had lapse and Crystal was about to push the bell again, and then Rosie open the door. With fake grins and greetings, they exchanged fake kisses inches away from their faces. Crystal complemented Rosie on her "pregnancy glow" saying she was jealous. Rosie asked if she wanted something to drink. Crystal replied saying she wanted some water with a wedge of lemon. Rosie said ok and headed towards the kitchen. Meanwhile, Crystal walked towards the mantle and reached in her handbag and took out the baby monitor, turned it on and placed it behind a picture frame. Crystal then continued pretending to admire Rosie's artwork. Then Rosie returns to the living room with the glass of water in hand and said "let's see what's in your goody bag my sistah ".

After about thirty minutes, Crystal had shown Rosie all the fragrances she had in her bag, and given her all the samples she had brought. Crystal then told Rosie that she had one more stop to make and didn't mean to rush. Rosie said she's having company over in about twenty minutes, and she was grateful for all the free samples. They exchanged fake kisses once more and Rosie escorted Crystal out the front door. As Crystal walks down the stairs, she says "I'll see you at church okay ". " Lords willing! " Rosie replied. Before Crystal opened her car door, she looked up the staircase at Rosie and with another fake grin, waves. Rosie replied with the same.

Crystal drove around the block a few times until she saw Tony pull up in front of Rosie's building. She then parked on the side of the building and waited for Tony to ring the bell. Then she turned on the baby monitor receiver, and reached for her iphone to record the conversation. The first words that came out of the receiver was "coming sweetie". Rosie opened the door and Tony was in. With a worried look on her face, Crystal sat in her car and listened. "Here's your jacket my love. You rushed out of here like a bat out of hell. I clearly forgot about the jacket until the next day. It's been about three month since you were last here". Tony agreed that it has been a while since that rainy night. He said he felt uneasy about what may have transpired that evening. Tony also mentioned he had a strange dream that rainy night, and it continued to bother him. He told Rosie he hoped that he was a gentleman during his drunkiness. She said he was definitely gentle and that she truly enjoyed herself.

Tony asked her about the male point of view she wanted to talk about. Rosie asked Tony to take a seat, and she had something important to tell him. But first she wanted to know what the dream was all about. Tony asked why she wanted to know. She said it may be connected to what she have to tell him. Tony told her it is quite embarrassing to talk about, but asked her not to think he was trying to [be with her] or subconsciously wanting to have sex with her. He said all he could remember was being helpless, with his hands restrained above his head, with a woman on top of him, her hair and hot breath touching his face,and riding him like a race horse. He also mentioned that this woman spoke fluent Spanish the whole time. Tony said it was somewhat realistic because after he woke up, he felt pretty drained. "Somehow things just didn't seem right" he said.

With a look of concern and worry on her face, Rosie confessed to Tony that they had made passionate love on that stormy night. She told him that he had seduced her, and she couldn't resist his advances. And because of it, she is now pregnant.

Chapter 2

With a look of disbelief on Tonys face, he stood up and covered his face with both hands. All Tony could say was "no, this can't be true". "You could of told me I seduced you that night Rosie"! "this can't be happening to me". "I knew something was wrong! You know I'm married, woman! Cora will certainly leave me and kill me. One word could have ended this whole thing....no!"

Now Tony, looking back at that stormy night when Rosie had that silly smirk on her face, coming out of the shower, realized it may have been a setup. The anger began to show on his face and Rosie knew Tony was getting angrier by the minute. As Tony expressed his disbelief about the situation, his voice was getting louder, then Rosie ask him to lower his voice and calm down. Tony then got up from his seat, quickly grabbed Rosie by booth arms and told her she must terminate the pregnancy.

With a soft demeanor, Rosie asked Tony to let her go, and to listen to her very carefully. He released her from his grasp and Rosie stood to her feet. She said she wasn't going to abort their baby. With her finger in his face, Rosie sternly informed Tony that she knew all about his affair with Crystal and he wasn't in a position to demand anything, and she had proof.

Meanwhile, in the car, with her mouth wide opened and her jaw dropped to her lap, Crystal couldn't believe what she was hearing. With her suspicion realized, Crystal continued listening.

"I don't care what proof you have, Crystal is my friend, just like I thought you were my friend. You had no right to take advantage of me". And then Tony says "you must be crazy". With eyes bucked and nose flaring, Rosie exclaimed, "as long as you live, don't you ever call me crazy! I hate that word!" "you're crazy!" Tony shouted.

Holding her stomach, and lips pressed firmly together, Rosie took a deep breath through her flaring nostrils and walked over to the entertainment center in the corner of the room. She pulled out a DVD and turned on the television and slid the disc into the DVD player. The first visual that popped up on the screen was the caption, "this is your loving husband". Then a video of Tony and Crystal sitting together at a restaurant, holding hands under the table, looking like the perfect couple, very much in love. As Tony quietly watched the video, Rosie asked how he was going to explain this to Cora. With his mouth twisted, Tony looked at Rosie, and didn't respond. "oh my goodness, look at us sweetie". Tony focused again on the video, and then he saw himself being ridden like a horse. Rosie was on top, moaning and speaking Spanish, her long hair draped over Tonys face. You could clearly see Rosie holding him down by his arms. Rosie was moving as fast as a race horse crossing the finish line.

"I've seen enough!" Tony exclaimed. With tears flowing down his face, Tony asked "what am I going to do now? If this gets out, I'll loose my wife, and a dear friend". Rosie tried to console Tony by putting her arms around him, but he pushed her away. "You know Cora will kick you to the curb once she finds out, or she may just stab you to death, either way you will be out of Cora's life forever. You know Tony, this is what need to do. You need to find a way to leave your wife. Cora will not stand for you having a love child with a fellow choir member. If you need help telling her, we can inform her together".

"you must be crazy!" Tony exclaimed. With lips pressed together and index finger pointed in towards the ceiling, Rosie hesitated for a couple seconds, and then walked back to the DVD player and pulled the DVD from the player and said, "since I'm crazy, I have the perfect excuse to show this lovely piece of work to Cora". At this point Tony snatched the DVD from Rosie and broke it into pieces. Rosie looked at him with amazement. "baby..... that was not the original. I have a special copy for your soon to be ex-wife, which would be just devastating to her health and emotional well being".

Tony knew she was right, Cora's health was failing because of her multiple sclerosis. With both hands in the air, Tony says, " I give up, you win. What do you want?". "Sweetie, I want you to be active in our child's life. You don't have to live with us right away, we can make a gradual transition. After you and Cora split and you get your own place, we can visit each other and see how it works out".

Tony paused for a long two minutes while Rosie watched with anticipation. While rubbing his face, Tony responded with, "I need time to think about this. I just need some time". "baby I know it's a lot to digest. Take as much time as you need. We will be here waiting".

In the car, with Crystal realizing the drama was just about over, she packs up her eavesdropping equipment and waited for Tony to exit Rosie's place. About three minutes later, Crystal observes Rosie opening the door. Tony crossed the threshold looking bewildered and confused. He slowly walked down the stairs, holding his head down as he walked towards his vehicle. Before getting in the car, Tony looked up at Rosie standing in the doorway. She nervously smiled and waved at Tony. As Tony drove away, Crystal sat there for a minute digesting what had just transpired, then drove off.

After his supposed [male point of view/retrieve jacket] meeting with Rosie, Tony drove around town for about an hour, stopping along the way to let the tears flow. All he could think about was the hurt that Cora would feel once she finds out, let alone the pain he would experience when his wife leaves him. And then there's Crystal, the sweet, pretty, young thing Cora and Tony agreed upon that would fill in the blanks in Tonys sex life. He thought he had the best possible situation any man could ever hope to have.

Tony then began to think about how and where to break the devastating news to Cora. He knew he didn't want to break the news at home, there was too many knifes in the kitchen, too many things to throw. Although Cora's health wasn't the best, Tony knew people under adversity can have super human strength. He even thought about texting Cora, but realizes that would be a cowardly move.

Tony pulls up in front of his home and sat there for a minute before going inside. There in the living room, relaxing on the chase lounge was Cora, reading a book. Tony approached his wife and gave her a passionate kiss, then another one, as though it would be the last kiss ever in life. Tony could smell dinner in the air. He could also smell a freshly bathed Cora, with Tonys favorite perfume on, Dolce & Garbana's Light Blue. Tony knew love making was in the air also. But making love was the furthest thing on his mind. Cora wasn't sexually aroused that often for the past couple of years and Tony knew she was horny. "how was your day baby" Cora asked softly. " "kind of rough sweetheart, not a good day" Tony says in a downhearted voice. With a look of concern Cora says"What's the matter baby? Ooh, your eyes are kinda puffy. Have you been crying?" "yea baby......I got so much on my mind". Once again Tony began to tear up. "I love you so much Cora, I really do". "I love you too baby, but what's the matter?" "Cora you know I wouldn't do anything to hurt you, right?" "you've been very good to me Tony. I couldn't ask for a better husband". "thanks baby" Tony replied. "does this have anything to do with Crystal?" "No, Crystal has nothing to do with this"

Then Cora's cell phone rang. She looked at the caller ID, noticing it was Crystal. She let the call go to voicemail, to call her back later. Then the house phone started to ring. It was Crystal again, Cora then picked up. " Hey Crystal what's up?" "Girl we need to talk, it's extremely important! Is Tony home?" "Yes he is". "Did He tell you what happened to him this evening?" "He's trying to tell me something but it's seems difficult for him girl" said Cora with frustration in her voice. "listen girlfriend, don't press him just yet, wait for me, I'm on my way!" Before Cora could ask a question, Crystal had hung up. Then the doorbell rang. Cora grabbed her cane and walked towards the door. "baby, Crystal is on her way. We can talk about it later". When she opened the door, there was nobody. But before closing the door, Cora noticed a small Avon shopping bag with a nicely wrapped package inside. A small card attached to it saying "Open at once! You need not be in the dark any longer".

Cora brought the package inside and quickly opened it. There was a DVD with a handwritten statement, "looks like your man is cheating on us". Cora expression changes as she looks at Tony mopping on the sofa. She limps over to the DVD player and inserted the disc. She watched intently as the video showed Crystal and Tony sitting at a table in a restaurant, holding hands under the table. Cora thought to herself "this ain't nothing new! But they shouldn't be holding hands in public. Crystal has some explaining to do". She kept watching, and then the damaging part of the disc appeared on the screen. Cora's mouth drops as she watches. Tony got up from the sofa and walked over to where Cora was, fixated on the TV screen. "WHAT THE HELL" Cora exclaimed. "Is that you? This can't be! Who is this Tony!" she shouted.

Then the doorbell rang. Tony walked quickly to the door as not to risk getting hit over the head with Cora's cane. He opened the door and there was Crystal . "Where's Cora" she asked. He got out of Crystals way, and she ran straight to Cora. "Girl look at this crap! This so-called husband of mine is screwing this whore!" Crystal held Cora's hands "Cora, I know it looks bad.... but this is not what it seem". "I guess he think he's a big time player since he has a friend on the side!" "That is simply not the case girlfriend. Your husband, my friend is being blackmailed......and guess who it is girl............"

Crystal began to tell the story, from suspecting Rosie's motives, to planting the baby monitor and listening in on the drama that unfolded in Rosie's apartment. Crystal pull out her cell phone and played back the drama that went down at Rosie's place. When Crystal was done with the story, Cora began to realize and understood why Tony had such a difficult time informing Cora about what had happened. Cora sat there on the sofa, in a daze. She grabbed her cane, got up from the sofa and looked around for Tony. "Sweetie" Cora called out. The front door was still opened. Crystal looked throughout the house,there was no Tony. They both noticed Tonys car was gone. Cora and Crystal tried calling him, but their call went straight to voicemail. They left messages asking him to come home as soon as he can. Tony returned Cora's phone call and said that he was going to spend a couple of days at a hotel to mentally work things out. He asked her not to worry, and that he would come home as soon as his head clears. Crystal and Cora sat there in the living room for the rest of that evening strategizing their next move.

About thirty minutes before Sunday service, Tony, with garment bag in hand, enters the choir assembly room and noticed Cora and Crystal sitting together, quietly talking. Most of the choir members were present except for Rosie. As Tony unzipped his garment bag to pull out his robe, Cora walked over to her husband

and asked, "can I help you with your robe". Tony replied "sure". As Cora helped her husband, she softly whispered "honey, if you feel up to it, can we have a talk? Me, you and Crystal? Tony, I am not angry with you at all. Perhaps we can discuss things over dinner at our favorite soul food restaurant, or any place you wish". "Rudy's Soul Food will be fine. What time should I be there?" "Is three ok" Cora asked. "Three will be fine Cora". Cora then kissed her husband on the lips and walked back to her seat and continued her conversation with Crystal. At that moment Rosie walked into the assembly room. She glanced at Tony as he sat in the corner of the room. He then looked away. As Rosie quickly walked towards the coat rack, Crystal rushed over to greet Rosie. "Hey girlfriend! Let me help you with your coat". "thanks Crystal but I'll really need help in my ninth month". "How many months are you now Rosie?" "Girl I'm six month, and three to go. I can't wait to deliver this baby boy". "It's a boy? That's great Rosie". "Have you thought about a name yet?" "I'm thinking about naming him after his daddy". "Girl you was suppose to tell me who's the baby daddy. I guess we had too much fun sampling those fragrances". "Yeah that was fun. Thanks for the freebies Crystal" Rosie says with a smile. "So who's the baby daddy girlfriend?" "I'll tell you after he ties up some loose ends with his soon to be ex-wife" Rosie whispered. "He's married?". "Yes he is Crystal, you'll be the first to know just as soon as his legal separation is final". An elderly choir member asked for silence and led everyone in prayer. Once the prayer was over, the choir began to exit the assembly room. Before entering the sanctuary, Rosie lagged behind so that she could have a word with Tony, "Tony" Rosie said softly, but he just passed her by. Rosie thought to herself "He don't look like a happy camper. Maybe he's angry about me sending the DVD a bit early. I had to do it so that Cora could kick him to the curb before our baby's born".

During the service, Cora would occasionally stare at Rosie. She couldn't help but notice Rosie's belly. Cora always wanted a child but couldn't conceive because of the multiple sclerosis medication. In the past, Cora and Tony discussed the possibility of using a surrogate and decided to ask Crystal in the near future. Now with Rosie in the picture, those plans seems to be going down the drain. Noticing Cora was fixated on Rosie, Crystal softly rubbed Cora's back and whispered "we'll turn these lemons into the best tasting lemonade ever, just you see girl". At that moment, with pain written on her face, Rosie left the choir loft holding her belly. "She seem to be having a ruff pregnancy Cora, looks like she's always in pain". "Yeah I noticed that too" Cora said in total agreement. After about ten minutes, Rosie reentered the sanctuary. She appeared to have been crying a bit, her eye liner was almost non-existent and eyes were puffy. Rosie looked towards Tony as she took her seat, and once again his eyes would have nothing to do with her. For the remainder of the service, Rosie had a sullen look on her face.

The after-church crowd at Rudy's Soul Food was present. Crystal and Cora arrived about fifteen minutes early so they could get a good booth. The aroma of fried chicken, collard greens, candied yams, fried catfish, pot roast, cornbread dressing and peach cobbler was in the air. And as always, some Ridgeway Baptist Church members were dining there. "You know, I really miss Tony these past few days. We haven't been apart for this long since we've been together" Cora said with sadness in her voice while fighting back the tears. "We will get through this situation Cora, I know we will. Rosie won't get away with this. Once we explain our plan to Tony, he'll see that this plan is a win-win situation for us". "For a brief moment in the choir room I almost forgot where I was. Girl.....while you were helping Rosie with her robe, all I wanted to do was beat the living daylights out of her. Right then and there, I had to pray and ask God to take away the desire to give Rosie the beat-down of a life time". "From here on Cora, you must keep your cool in order for this plan to work, no beat-downs, ok?" "yeah ok, no beat-downs.....Crystal you're no fun". "Hey, there's Tony" says Crystal as she waves at him. As he walk towards the booth, Cora and Crystal had the biggest smile any man would ever want to see. "Hey baby, I'm glad you could make it" says Cora as Tony gave her a kiss on the lips. As Tony sat down next to his wife, he grasped Crystals hands "And how are you my dear friend?". "I'm doing fine Tony , but the important question is, how are you? We were a bit worried about you". "There's no need to worry ladies, I just needed time to sort things out, clear my head, that's all. I am totally famished. What are we having? I haven't had a good meal in a while".

The three of them ate well. Before, dessert was served, Cora and Crystal began to ask Tony some very important questions. They picked his brain on subjects such as family, children and the what-ifs in life. Tony was intensely engaged in the discussion. "What if Rosie won't......." and "that sounds good but what if......". Tony had many questions and some couldn't be answered. At the end of their get-together, all three were laughing, and it seem they were all on one accord. Tony asked the waitress for the check and Crystal immediately offered to pay. "I got this y'all. The food was awesome and this meeting of the minds was very productive. So.... it sounds like we have a plan.... right?" Cora and Tony simultaneously said "It's a plan".

A week later, Rosie returned home from work to find a invitation in her mailbox. It read "You are invited to your baby shower. It will be held at the Embassy Suite Hotel, Lombard, Illinois, suite 1002. Be there at three o'clock Saturday. If you have any questions call me, Crystal at 777- 1428, see you there!". With a big grin, Rosie thought to herself "That Crystal isn't so bad after all. I kinda like the chick". Rosie walked down the hall to the spare bedroom. She opened the door and there was a new baby bed, a rocking chair, a changing table and all the things a new mother would want to have for her baby. She laid the invitation on the changing table. Rosie sat in the rocking chair, held her head back, held her belly and began to rocked.

At Wednesday's choir rehearsal, Tony seemed more relaxed then he did before the dinner meeting at Rudy's. Rosie was still trying to get eye contact with Tony, but he never looked in her direction. Cora was still cordial toward Rosie. Crystal was even more gracious then Cora. Once rehearsal was over and the choir members began to exit the loft, Rosie made sure she was the last female to leave the loft. Because Rosie knew Tony would be the perfect gentleman. He always allowed all the female members to exit first. When all the women had finished exiting the loft, Rosie and Tony was face to face. "Hey Tony, how have you been?" as she reaches to hug her baby daddy. Tony had no other choice but to hug Rosie. It wouldn't look kosher if he had rejected her. With an awkward expression on his face, Tony responded "I'm doing fine Rosie. How about you?" Holding her belly, "we are doing just fine, thanks for asking". "Hey girlfriend, what's going on?" Crystal says as she interrupts and saves Tony from what had to be agonizing for him. "A baby shower is what's going on girl. And I will be there before time, ok" Rosie says with confidence. "By all means, please do" Crystal replied. "I can't wait to see our little bundle of joy Rosie.

As Rosie drove to the baby shower, she couldn't help but think about her baby. She daydreamed about Tony playing ball with his son in the backyard, throwing him up in the air, then catching him and Tony along with herself, standing in the doorway of their sons bedroom, watching him sleep. Rosie also fantasizes about how Tony would come around and accepts the fact that they are now a family, and Tony asking for her hand [on bended knee, of course] in marriage. "Turn right onto Butterfield Road" the GPS prompted Rosie. "In point one miles you will arrive at your destination.....Your destination is to the right". Rosie thought to herself "this is a nice hotel". She then pulled into a parking spot in front of the hotel.

Chapter 3

Rosie walked through the revolving door and looked up and all around. She couldn't help but think to herself "this is a beautiful hotel." Then her stomach began to hurt once more. Holding her stomach, Rosie pauses for a few seconds while holding her belly, then continued towards the front desk. "May I help you ma'am?" With a big smile Rosie answers "Yes, I'm here for my baby shower.......suite 1002." After looking up the room, the front desk person directed her to the elevators.

Once on the tenth floor, Rosie took her time walking to the suite. When she arrived at 1002, Rosie knocks twice. The door opened, standing there was Tony, with a fake grin. Rosie was speechless. She stood there with amazement. And then Tony asked, "are you coming in?" Rosie quietly interred the suite. There was no baby shower decorations in the suite what so ever. When she got to the middle of the room, she heard the door locked behind her. She looked behind her and there stood Cora and Crystal. They both had stern looks on there faces. Cora walked towards Rosie while Crystal remained at the door. With a look of concern on Rosie's face, she nervously asked "I guess there's no baby shower today? ". Sarcastically Cora replied "take a load off Rosie " as she pointed to a chair that was positioned in the middle of the room. Rosie slowly took her seat. By the look of the faces in the room, Rosie knew she was in big trouble. Tony grabbed another chair and placed it in front of Rosie. Cora then sat down and looked at Rosie with disgust. Cora handed the cane to her husband as not to strike Rosie with it. Cora looked up at the ceiling and took a deep breath and said under her breath "Lord help me ". Then she looked at Rosie straight in the eyes and asks "Now Rosie, I have three questions to ask you. Be truthful with me because I don't have much patience right now. At this stage of my life, I really don't want to catch a case.........if you know what I mean" Rosie looked at Tony, standing next to Cora. She began to stand up, but Crystal immediately pushed her back down to her seat. Cora asks "Do you know why you're here? " With a confused look on Rosie's face " my baby shower? " Cora gestured for the cane but Tony replied " not now baby " as he starred emotionless at Rosie. Cora exclaimed "Who's the baby daddy? " With a bowed head and a sullen look on her face, Rosie replied "I couldn't refuse Tony's advances! Your husband is so irresistible! He kept hitting on me and I just gave in! " "That's BS and you know it! " Cora shouted. "It's true Cora! I wouldn't lie to you! " While still standing behind Rosie, Crystal pulled out her cell phone and began to playback the conversation she had recorded at Rosie's apartment.

When Rosie heard the first two sentences, she knew the jig was up....game over. At first, she had a blank look on her face and then it turned into a look of concern. All she could do was shield her belly with her arms. "Please don't hurt my baby! He's all I have! What ever you want me to do, I'll do! But please don't hurt my baby! " By now the tears had begun to flow down Rosies face. She was visibly stunned. With a trembling voice, she cried out "oh help me God! "

Cora, Tony and Crystal all looked at each other, then they focused again on Rosie. With a stern look on her face, Cora took a deep breath and says "I have a mind to take this to the police. " Rosie cried out. "Police! " "Yes police...... you raped my husband girl! " "Oh my god Cora, I didn't think of it as rape! " says the mother to be. "Yes, it definitely was rape. We had it checked out by a prosecutor friend of ours. " At this point, Rosie's tears started flowing profusely. She was still protecting her belly with her arms and had begun to rock back and forth in her chair. "You know Rosie, we can make this all go away. Tony and I have a plan, a very good plan. There will be no need for you to do any jail time.

Besides, they just love pretty girls like you in prison. Now listen carefully. Tony and I always wanted a child of our own. I cannot conceive because of the multiple sclerosis. It pains me to think that I will never have a child of my own. I prayed and prayed but to no avail. I guess it wasn't meant for me to conceive a child.........Again Rosie, listen carefully........ I want a written statement of what happened that night......and we want you to sign it also. Plus..... we want to videotape the statement as well. " With both hands, Rosie wiped tears from her face. Her eyeliner was smeared around the eyes. " honey, give Rosie some water.....she doesn't look so well. " Tony nods yes. The demoralized Rosie took a drink of water. "I've already asked God to help make room in my heart for forgiveness..........but it is so hard. " Cora then leaned forward to grab Rosie by the hand and looked eye to eye and asked softly" I'd like to raise the baby as my own. I will take very good care of him.........I promise. " "You want to raise my son? I have big plans for this baby. " says the sobbing Rosie. "Tony and I will allow you to watch us raise the boy from afar. We are very much open to that. Then later on........maybe you can become more involve with the child. Besides, the child does have your DNA.........and we.......Tony and I......will be financially responsible OUR child. " Then the bottle of water Rosie was holding hit the floor. She slumped over to the side, her head tilted back. Crystal held Rosie as to not let her fall on the floor. " Call 911! " Cora shouted.

At the University of Chicago Hospital, Cora, Tony and Crystal, waited for word on Rosie's condition. There was a look of sorrow on their faces. They've been waiting for three hours. Tony paces the floor. They barely spoke a word to each other. The three of them stood to their feet as the emergency room physician walked through the double doors. With a serious look on the doctor's face, he asked, "Are you all the next of kin of Rosie Sanchez. " "No. We have been looking through her cell phone trying to find her relatives, but we couldn't find any. We belong to the same church. Rosie sings with us in the choir. All we know is she's from Puerto Rico. " The physician explains that Rosie is in and out a diabetes related coma and that the baby seem to be doing fine except for a little stress and said that he will monitor baby closely as well. The physician asks do they know who's the baby's father. Tony informed the doctor that he is the father and he wanted to be notified when there is a change in her condition.

After three weeks, family services still could not find Rosie's next of kin. She was still in intensive care. Tony and Cora visited Rosie every day. They prayed and talked to Rosie while she lie motionless. It was obvious Cora and Tony was very concerned about Rosie's state of being. They spoke to Rosie as though she could hear them. At the end of each visit, Tony and Cora would put their hands on Rosie's belly, praying and trying to feel the baby kicks. Every time they would feel some movement, Cora and Tony would look at each other with amazement.

After Sunday's service, Rudy's Soul Food restaurant was once again was full of patrons. Cora and Tony, waiting to be seated, noticed Crystal sitting in a booth alone. Crystal looks up from the menu and spots Tony and Cora smiling at her. She gestured for them to join her, and they did. "You didn't tell me you were going to be eating here! " "Girl, you know I can't cook. This will be the best meal I'll have all week. " Crystal says as she chuckled. "Well Crystal, I haven't been much in the mood for cooking lately since what happened to Rosie. She's really been on my mind. " "Me too" Crystal says with concern. Then Tony's phone rings. "Hello....yes it is................ really!..........ok, we'll be right there! " "Is everything okay? " Cora asked with concern. "Baby we have to get to the hospital right now! " Tony says as he napkin's his lips and pays for the meals.

At the intensive care unit, Crystal, Tony and Cora stood there behind the glass, watching Rosie being attended to by two doctors and a nurse. One doctor appears to be talking to Rosie, seemingly having her follow his finger with her eyes. The other doctor spots Cora and Tony and exited the room. "We got here as fast as we could. Is Rosie okay? What about the baby? " Tony says with extreme concern on his face. " Well Mr. and Mrs. Mansfield.....I have some very encouraging news. First, the baby is doing just fine. Secondly, Rosie has started to speak....... and man did she speak! At first, we could not make out what she was saying. Then she started asking for Tony and Cora, over and over again. And then, she kept saying.....take care of my baby ,please take care of my baby..... You all can talk to Rosie for only a short time. She is very weak and we don't want to stress her." The doctor then escorted Tony and Cora to Rosie's bedside. Her eyes were barely open."Looks like you have guests Rosie " the doctor says with excitement, then looked at Cora and Tony. "They're only going to be here for a few minutes so that you can get your rest." "Sure" Tony responded. Cora sat down in a chair next to the bed while Tony stood by his wife's side. Rosie slowly turned her head towards Cora. "I am so sorry.......for what I have done. I'm very ashamed. Tony........If only I could take that night back.......but I can't. I took advantage of you......... and that was wrong." Cora tries to interject but Rosie slowly lifts her hand. With a raspy voice she says " let me finish". Cora looked up at Tony and then back down at Rosie. " I dreamt that you and Tony prayed for me.........and the baby. I could see myself lying in this bed.......... with you and Tony standing over me. I felt like.... God's presence filled room. Then I saw a bright light on the other side of the room......... and I knew God was near. So I prayed and asked God to give me more time so that I can apologize to you and Tony for what I have done and to let you know that yes........ you can raise our little boy." With tears in her eyes, Cora held Rosie's hand and says "thanks..... thank you so very much." "You all will be great parents........ I just know it." Suddenly, Rosie's eyes started moving erratically and her mouth opened wide. The alarms on the monitors began to sound and the medical team rushed in. Tony and Cora was hurried out of the room.

Meanwhile in the waiting room, Crystal waited patiently. Rosie was very much on her mind. Then Cora and Tony walked through the door, they were visibly shaken. " what's the matter?" Crystal says with concern. "Rosie had regained consciousness........she wanted to apologize........." With tears in her eyes, Cora began to recount everything that transpired in the intensive care unit. Tony did his best to comfort his wife but Cora kept crying.

Three hours had past and no word on Rosie's condition. Cora's head was laying on Tony's shoulder as they sat on the sofa. Crystal returning from a coffee run, had three cup of java and some snacks in hand. As she passes the coffee to her friends, the ICU physician interred the waiting room. The three listened intensely to the physician as he explained what was going on with Rosie. He explained that Rosie experienced a brain aneurysm and she is undergoing an operation to stop the hemorrhaging. The surgery may take up to eight hours. But he also explained that he had to give Rosie an emergency cesarean section to save the baby. The doctor then told them he would be back with more information on

Rosie's procedure.

    While they wait for word on Rosie's condition, the three walked to the nursery to view their bundle of joy. There he was, in an incubator being attended to by two nurses. Tony and Cora smiled at each other, then continued admiring their little preemie.

    Three years later, Crystal had [two years prior] moved in with Tony and Cora to assist them with T.J. [Tony Jr.], and also to help Cora with her declining health. Their relationship has never been better. Tony and Crystal's relationship has grown as well.

    At the kitchen table, Crystal and Cora reminisced about the past. They were both laughing and giving each other high fives. Cora picked up her cane and walked towards the picture window, Crystal soon followed. "T.J. is certainly a split image of his father". Crystal says with amazement while watching Tony playing with his son. And then the doorbell chimed. "Who could this be?" asks Crystal as she walk towards the door. When Crystal opened the door, she could not believe what she was seeing. Cora looked astonished as well. There was Rosie, standing there with a gift bag in one hand and a cane in the other.

THE   END